What Santa Can't Do

NORTH POLE

To all of Santa's
helpers, big and small
— D. W.

To one of Santa's
best helpers, Linda C.
— D. C.

What Santa Can't Do

by **Douglas Wood**   pictures by **Doug Cushman**

Simon & Schuster Books for Young Readers

New York   London   Toronto   Sydney

There are lots of things that regular people can do, but Santa can't.

Santa can't drive a car.
(That would hurt the reindeer's feelings.)

And he can't fly in airplanes.
(That would *really* hurt their feelings!)

Santa can't do his best work without elves.

And he can't wait to try out the new toys!

Santa just can't help smiling.
And he can't seem to smile without his eyes twinkling.

He can't *stand* having an empty lap.

Santa can't chuckle. Or giggle. Or snicker.
He can only "Ho! Ho! Ho!"

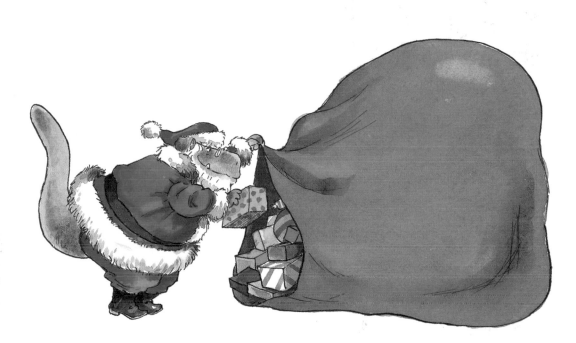

He can't pack a regular suitcase.

He can't come into a house the normal way.
He doesn't know how doorknobs work.

Santa doesn't really like fires in fireplaces. ("Ouch!")

He just can't seem to walk past a plateful of cookies.
Or a glass of milk.

And he can't leave a single gift in his bag,
even the tiniest one.

There are lots of things Santa can't do.
Lots of ways he's different.
But in one way he's just like you and me.

He can't *wait* for Christmas!